Above the Mountain

ABOVE THE MOUNTAIN

W. David Smith

[POEMS]
2013

Bristlecone Peak Books
Midway, Utah

Portions first published in
A PASSAGE THROUGH THE ROCKIES
by
Galena Press
Denver, Colorado
1984

Library of Congress Control Number: 2013939402

ISBN 978-0-9893753-1-3
[E-book edition]

ART: *The Thatched Hut of Dreaming of an Immortal*

T'ang Yin (1470-1523) China, Ming Dynasty
Details, courtesy of the Freer Gallery of Art, Smithsonian
Institution, Washington, D.C.

For Jerilyn

Thank you
Anhui and Central Washington Universities, Deseret News,
Norman Dubie, Freer Gallery of Art of the Smithsonian Institution,
Galena Press, Greyhound, Brewster Ghiselin, Christine and Michael
Kerner, Betsy Kohut, Jerilyn S. McIntyre, Kim Mercer, Warren and
Elizabeth Street, Allen Tilley, the Universities of Iowa and Utah,
and other folks I've met, in person and in books.

Views and errors herein are my own or those of fictive characters.

Contents

I. So Here You Are

Sam's Repairs

"Shine 'em up here, kid.
Stay off the streets."

Shoes both-sides broken of walking weight,
'50s wedgies glowing like a shirt-rubbed plum,
        small saddle correctives,
a sailor's oxfords two-months forgotten, for sale,
a single worn high-platform —

[10]   war-wounded to a walkless catcher's stance,
            Sam tossed the last, a mechanic's boot
            new-heeled and stitched,
                to the high-up
        worn pine counter with the rest

and, where a gob of rubber glue stuck,
thumb-rubbed a Singer logo for luck.

Outcast

The path came apart
beneath the lower lake,
and the boy saw the outcast
seated beneath a tree, chanting
his hand along the ground.
He was stroking a footstep with his thumb,
not changing it, though the soil
darkened slightly as if he
were roughing the underside of leather.

"What are you doing?" asked the boy.
The outcast stopped.

     "One is lost."

Great Salt Lake 1963

Sun-drained for eons
and little time left,
        science said,
for even I shall stand
on the salt flat depths
of that waterless sea:

Black Rock
lone chunk
two barns high
on crusted beach
like a brain let out
to see for itself
the lake's life receding.

        No flies light.

You cannot know
such cleanliness
eating incunabula
from celluloid
in white libraries
with your eyes
as I did to forget
how that strangling sea
strangled me at seven
when swimming I dared to become
        its one living subject.

        O fallacy! This is
a dead world, you say.
Yet on Black Rock Beach
a thing of red-tide salt
not only touched but parched
sinuses sting-dried eyes

into blanched nuts
and brain lobes throbbed
in prism-white sight
yes that *makes* sense:

How little now
the border of your being
becomes my being —
little more dries blood
into hard brown-
red deserts each
          in a vein
microcosmic:

[13]

how grateful I am
to the Many Lifetimes
          for this fact:

at seven I became a pillar of salt
          sodden, sobbing
yearned for salt-measured palmsful

          salt
of this crystalline sea
          and water

Rivers Jordan, Weber and Bear

empty into allegory

"He who receives all and gives none
          will end as this"

no slaves for ages digging 'til dead,
no salt wars since before Huangdi —

this trapped land
called promise

mountain after desert after mountain after

salt, salt lake

no water
water smelter smoke

rainbow swimming out, out
of Weber as if to sea
        surges

brown into fuchsia

drinks and strangles as I

nothing to save
no backturning

only this:
        recover

(catfish fast back
into Jordan, laughing
toward some muddy Galilee,
like the grown folks surrounding me,
to their knees in nothing, laughing)

        what centuries cannot

(brine shrimp do live
gathered in hoards
for brine shrimp in hoards
for brine flies
for seabirds in hoards

with wings heavy with salt

some cannot fly but walk solemn
salt-heavy wings out

    flap slow
        in the deep sun—

feathered hulk
with eyes out
for flies in small bites)

I stand on Black Rock knowing

how little
I fit in this cycle
where things
    of great cycles
end in a cycle and

Doom
becomes me, us.

Yes. And for all
though the patience
    of rain
falls to our eyes

we cannot sleep sleep.

    This jubilee
        of nevers
            trills dreams—

sundown's shadow
leaches these dreams

and we of the West know
the perverse face of promise

catching rivers for crops
rivers leaching to that great sea

lost on flats
in these last days —

(a valley away died
a gassed lamb)

we the salt of that earth

Leaving

Not until desert clouds at sunset
        blow with mortality
and the hands of amber change
your hand a sudden moment:

        care for this house,
                for I must go.

                Don't stay beyond love
                or memory's strain.   [17]

Night Song

Laughter's ghost
climbs the mind
like jackboots in loose ore.

Now hope seems only
what might have been.

Once between the hours
long ago, we laughed
away loving
with nothing but hope,
too young to name
its distances of parting.

I see you now in dreams
and after can't sleep off
your way of being.

Crimes of rain
erode hot as blood
through deeper sleep,
through this my weak eyes' seeming:

Never now the losses we share —
what's left of questions and laughter.
In the yearning hour of night
a book-weary love calls:

The different song beneath the strain
sifts through washing rock
like water: sweet, bitter.
We've become people
we didn't know.

When an ore shard
becomes my heart
and its powder sifts
its old thin giving
to tips of fingers only seeing,

still in darkness
you will not leave me.

[19]

Search

What is night hides:

Too long for tears —
calm through the glass
Jersey damp August
sparse crickets
tires hissing through water:

As if from pine barrens

[20]

she cries
so long

from somewhere

Crossing

It is the time when you sleep
to return slowly to nowhere:
a place you knew only
by passing through
and were still and watching:

Where you came from
hunts you; you have escaped,
your blood drained in solitude and thrown away.

It is the time of walking
the back road at night
through the barking of dogs,
it is the time of three roadways,
it is the time of the dropped limb.

Shrikes race down the canyon;
you swim out to the back
of the island; you are warm
and hear only your name.
It is the time for waking:

      You cannot.

Moths and Spiders

Moon turned lepidoptera
by edict of oak. Flight:
      tiny hands dancing.

In wraiths' glen —
      how we were
maundering: Light was licking
our quaking thighs
            (ladies
      alone, were we alone?)
as in Delvaux' *Venus Asleep.*
    Bones passed,
        moon-frozen mauve.
    Pray give, give.

*   *   *

Moon turned arachnid
by edict of stars. Hunt:
      Run to the touch.

In leaves of glen
I spin clean sheets,
waiting for him to arrive.
      Arrive. Him to arrive.

I yearn,
light-lovely moth,
      for you. You

Once in Stardust

Tumbleweeds taste of mine tailings to the pith:
catch one as they pitch, sift
down three streets east
      out of Stardust.

      Stardust, in Utah:
tumbling sews seeds
along the brittle drift.

I grew 'til time
in skins of wind
lurched down
smoke-scorched mountains
      and I left the place.

Yes, there's a home,
all ya need to know.

No one knows Joe Hill,
disorganized a decade
when my grandfather came

to Zion's land
to start again, once again
with visions and coal dust.

So here you are,
      dust from a star.

Joe Hill hangs in a blood-dobbed
boarding-house quilt,
threatening even me.

Listen don't talk
when ice-wind hammers

shrink anvils, and all seems
        where Doom looked:

Joe's pencil stub is squeaking still —
hokey tune, 'salt-n-pepper for the truth.'

At nights Joe and he tumble,
        all foxfire,
caught in the same draft,

each thinking he's Jacob,
                or the Voice itself.

I resist that wind,
my roots too loose.

Bus Station at Banks

When in Banks I found myself
and half none else
with shaking ankles cold
without the walls of Navidad
and paced a backward walk
as once the train
would take the ground
away. The frozen hound
      hung on the bus
quailed like the shaking dalmation
hunched by cold-blood brick
      and I
in 4 a.m. tungsten light

      exhausted

dry all eight fingers propped
on ribbed aluminum,

      unshaken,
      hounded,
      about.

Eyes' blood
numb to exile,
mounted,
the ticket
my given talent.

Banks, Oregon 1974

II. Journey of the Nails

Roadside Lights

I

The onset awake only
between self-seeming and seem

      Eastern sun
carnelian and garnet

Flatlands, winter wheat,
       light wind
            cantabile

Earthborn
      moon sliding long—

A sigh
      down long bajadas
          of alluvial dream.

II

Half-read books she said

"All of them are but half read

boxes in my mother's attic
are full of them"

stopped and forgotten
bright thread markers

[29]

at halfway

"for I must have
some other love today."

III

Meeting doubles
at commons tables

nod to me
in ambiguity

and the day
comes crispy with chips.

On the back porch
dogs nose the garbage.

We know
the comfort of distrust
and trust the ebb tide
feast of gulls.

And a dawn
holding for one
dissolves for all,
living the ages

      cast back to the living

unheard the ram's horn
and moments gone.

Can one heal one
not lost in the trying:
from a journey-less journey
      can love reach again?

IV

Fast as thought,
fox-tale barley
climbs a sleeve
like an awl of bird bone—

    wind plants barley.

V

Noon whistle —

whole den yapping.
Nose in her shadow,
coyote walks
to the shack.

Lunchbox, us.

[32] Right, she has
no wish to please.

VI

She woke up
and asked to be lifted
from the roadway dream:

She was naked in Lithia Park
as pinion cracked from the chimneys:
        she was in Ashland;
she was clothed with the hillside;
        she flew above the mountain
and nestled among soft cars   [33]
                like lambs on the roadway:

She was naked at the pond and families
feeding the half-white mallards
snapping through ranks
        watched her.

                She was
naked, feeding the roadside stag.
I licked sleep from her palm.

        I new her when
she had such dreams.

VII

As when you were five,
an almost when your voice
at last reached the distance
of what you could see,
and thus, goodbye?
Tact lands like a javelin.

Wind sings:

[34]   bronze and elder.

By Chance

Forgotten: a glass between us
and years in which the past
has dropped away in stones and silence
to hide like concrete under asphalt,
a crumble of bricks beneath.

And I wonder that
a road would cross at all,
following as in some places in the East

a path bent on hiding
change and lamentation
from only yesterday.

Now a circle arches in space
to grace a daytime's last light,
and so much, how much lost
with yesterday's forms flying a thermal
up the backbone of the mind?

This will take us
to the next of sevens:
Well, doing well.

Lost in the daylight
of common praises
the heart awakens to bliss
no longer — someone gone,
a wished-for lover you passed in a hallway
on the way to hope and knowing.

A past between two undoes itself
less easily than a lie;
what you have found between us
I'd want to find and will,

when passing is not the past
and book dust, blown
behind you, before me.
In another light doubtless
the thing would seem common:
mints on an after-dinner tray,
a glass beforehand,
the grand once-again.

Yet I try to find you now,
if in thought only,
time's scars like smiles about our eyes.

With one tongue, speaking many voices
and no emptying, but of when.

Magicicada

      Closed eyes
abstract the day:
beyond the river
a chorus tree
voice-heavy.

*

Cicadas bow
the locust branches,
neighbor-hated,   [37]
listening.

*

Breaking cantilena,
scolding,
not wishing
to be held.

*

Little heart,
you did not understand.
So like a cicada,
needing flight at third-song.

*

Eyes like coral,
wings of Zoas:
brooding dew
in the tree.

      From this land
the ice judge
has stolen
the cicada.

Ten with Tammy

One day came crying
when Tammy, I tried
to put you by.

Two days came lying
come find us the way
hands lettered by Mendel
broke bread to repay.

[38] Tettix, my love, on the third;
cicadas in a shoebox
wear eucalyptus,
pennyleaf for a hat.

These for thy mind's crying —
cry, child,
a step will be that.

Four days' rayless weft
of the ogives,
jussive, obtrusive.

Something between us
like a child
who could not speak,
had no needs,
could not be seen.

Three days' meeting,
five apart.
Three hearts. Three hearts.

Tammy twirls the sixth,
a practiced apotheosis
lata tata

swimming on land
a calico cat.

Calico town outside.
Inside, seven go
down Ghost Town Road,
slow.

Tammy's grace of eight's
bower of dalliance,
riven venation of sleep and back:
time is outside: memory
spaceless save in blinking:
space is inside.

[39]

Nine:
clouds shape the light of evening
above, below.
Step:
one helix, two —
ten billion step.

A matchstick
twirls between finger and thumb
to church bells and raga: a candle.

Tammy is waltzing
who say when:
who say when.
who say when,
who say when?
who say when —
who say when

One lynx,
ten martins:
lynx gone.

Tammy is saying,
"Stay, 'lest nature be wasteful."

Cardinal drops
through odd shapes of leaves
to red-berry moonseeds —
hour-long whistling her in.
Wing-clatter half-strains,
twelve moons on the ground.

Discontent with identity
I need her not for these,
            but for me.

When she is free.

Tauros

"Their words handle their lives
          so awkwardly" —

Tauros in Minos,
          sun on the wall's rim.

          "and I who must follow behind,
sight running ten times before the act,
          wanting only stillness."

[41]

Nostalgia

Like clams at lunch
my old eyeglasses
lounge around a drawer
dining on dust.

III. Bring

A Bowl of the Fremont,
Bear River

Marsh hawk drops,
curving through mist
beyond the river's bow
into night, and silence
before a voice:

I knew my hunger and you.
We are the broken bowl.
Core of two spirals
that never meet,
though they curve near.

Beginning, ending
as they ever were.

Ice harvests the bulrush.
The greasewood's lent of cells
closes the outward ring
dense as heartwood:
clouds turn rose spring
chalcedony, blown
through deepening blue.

If After Loving

But not without you
I found what would come to be,
surrounded your thousandth heart
with what might hold in the absence of you
          transfixed —

if I had not found the heart,
if war-anger had not unfolded into life.

Kindness was the slowness of other hands:
after from ages of distance and other lives to keep,
and now, when all is the promise
          of what life left will give us,
what making and loving will bring,
what seed beyond the next,
and beyond, past lovers kind in parting,
          knowing what can never part—

I knew the hurt of returning impossible
without you. If after loving, tears,
the moment cannot stop
          to wash away.

Long Ago, a Tree

> — *Limbs wandered alone.*
>   — Empedocles

Climb after catkin fall to find
carving in bark soft as muskmelon,
pale green-gray, the letters
cut in, whiter than pine, high up:

"We carved you up that tree
            with her, and you can't even see it."

I left them in an ammo-box clubhouse
with the musky smoke of cattail cigars
and bewildering cards from overseas

alone to shinny and slide back down
the tree, panting, with a knife in the teeth
lifted from the kitchen, sick
of being smallest, set to change—

at last to climb, glance and pass
where their bravery had stopped—
over those initials and bark brushed green—
            up through down-thick leaves
far over the wood stack, house
and chicken coop, huffed and crawled
to where barn owls chortled at midnight,
            and I the first human there.

When height had no more daring
I found an outward branch
            and backrode the wind
                in a whirl of sparrow chirrups,
and drifted in sun and leaf light

until the dream ran out
and I looked to the ground
to the neighbor girl slapping the tree
to be known and the distant
     "Come down!"

The mountains a band
of otherness unreachable
along the western sky:
climb the wood pile beneath after war
to watch the open-air train,
     a rusty-car Cathay,   [47]
roll to the crossroad,
the couplings crashing
in number to a last clump.

I caught one-handed
a lead soldier and wave
     from the engineer,
and hitched once free,
a hand up the chest-high step,
     and a *chush* became a rumble
speeding the flickering trees.

* * *

     Clogged daydreams
from boyhood and sudden loss —
climb and the house flies through the mind:

How long it takes to forget
one summer of becoming —
from letters in a tree to light
halved, adrift in the sick girl's hair
through leaves though she is gone
with my childhood also suspended in earth
'til loss split the root like sudden age:

I dreamed her again beneath the tree,
her silent parents like clouds
but stilled with life's weight,
                    lost ones before her,
            edge of the underground.

Sun and shadow swirl
                    on her shoulders:
she weighed my life,
            glanced, and went.

[48]   * * *

                    The tree does not hide behind its honesty,
            beyond its own politic,
does not seek the best attitude always,
come down from itself and walk away,
seeking solitude. The first
            high, thick-bark trunk
squat with many branches,
beyond itself underground:
                    white poplar root *omphalos*
and balance of earth and water beyond
to light — no whole seed, new growth
            only by break, drift, search.

In the synapse a spark,
            from the ray a day of crossing,
the tree run under ditch bank and track,
matching sun search out of the southern sky.

Almost matched in shared transfer —
            the lead-root cannot be a leaf.

Unfolded book and blood
            beneath in a hand
and across the synapse,

light wakes.
Dream a requiem if you can —
the night seeks no message
grown words can make.
    Were the message from silence,
finding would be of other times
each always, all never the same.
      In the back reaches of the sea,
the mind rises to set and rise
as the moon does, moving
    toward it through mountains.

[49]

* * *

The track was taken up:
the dawn sun chromelight
and rust on the rails,
two rows of workmen
striking spike mauls
to the crow "brawk"
of drawn spikes —

an hour I watched,
    half-a-day dog-barked orders
and rails speared the length
    of stooping silhouettes
    and rose, dropped *clang* on a greasy flatcar:
railroad ties craw-barred out of streambed gravel
like yanked-up spuds.

Told to stay away,
I stumbled back along the cattails
an irrigated field length,
the plowed ground dry,
too rough for walking,
sun-warped barn
marking the distance,

going down on its own.
Then nothing
to stay away from
but cinders and thought.

* * *

A tree in autumn
          does not wait for wind
                    to ease its sleep.

[50]   * * *

Light-fall in after-dawn
wakes on pages in a silent room:

The mind abroad maps flat a constellation,
          finds a lily's cross, passes
          to bike five miles for catfish
and come back blistered,
empty a wet gunnysack—
          fin-spikes caught, tails curled dainty
          'til the sudden thrash:

Life in silence, Plato's cave
and wonder's wake. The classes
of other faces, the gesture never
tracked to its end: habited silence
wondering at beginnings
never so simple: 'What am I next?'
          when a day was for making
          and life so easily won.

* * *

Her face I can't see,
her hands beneath the voice

folded light on brocade.
Child be with me,
the shadow is kind —
as when embers of a campfire
gutted almost beyond afterglow
and rose on the moment
of a wish, an unlost ember.

* * *

Fremont Island, Great Salt Lake,
        in fifty-mile wind —
at the top only the rocks survive,
        scant grass and a child
                trying to stand up —
                        steps, sudden and stunned.

* * *

The last dish stacked silent in the flour barrel,
the clothes pressed for the last time
for a year and folded away, wagon bound.
        We reach in other light
        and would will a day's
        remembrance and close,
spark in an engram,
the book replaced.

One learns to listen to the least,
late, as the light leads out.

The house is closed, the house
is closed, and find another.
The heart lets the past escape
in a breath, neighbor,
child and friend.

"I am crossing the plains
and the one thing I'll take
will be a skillet—
        "I am crossing the plains
and the one thing I'll take
will be a hen—
        I am crossing the plains
of the circle game
and into the Rockies,
        the children walking,
        sick or gone,
the wagon borrowed,
the wheel hubs worn.

The night train rumbles its stream of lights
beneath, above the canyon floor
and creek pale amber in the long reach
of dusk, and the stag turns the herd on the heights
away from the Great Basin sunset, promontory line,
        and back to a midway ridge bed
                in tall grass and darkness.

The willows bend in happenstance.
The loves unfold and vanish
        and want strips away want.
June's a day for traveling
alone with the sunset.

Cosmos spark, generations
in the dance of airwaves
to keep on seeking, keep.

The only trees river cottonwoods—
        dust swept from the log step
of a clay-bank house and miles to town.
                Small hands shown how to play.

A mountain moves in truckloads
to crush, wash and fire:
copper sheets arm-span wide
sheer clean from cathodes,
drop, stack flat for the melt.
Copper ingots stretch for miles,
link with lasers and glass.

* * *

An age finds hurt for the next:
voices gathered in millions
gone in a breath's inflection.

Win and divest the self,
take and take no other.
Jungled in the dead grounds
of broken pallets and boxcars,
a man, lumped in a leaf-dusty army
blanket, stilled with a boy's rock.
.
A boy on the highway, in the jungle, stilled.
Retreating stairs of sound in the hallway
        climb back, retreat.
I'll be back when the dawn
        cuts my fingers
as I lift her from the stairs
            in broken glass.
From the stairs the dawn lifts
        her own way; her hand slices
            along the rough staircase wall.

The light when I died
spoke the ocean's name.

        The ocean had day on her tongue.

We step from the nets
dominions cast—

the nets within them.

* * *

I return in the dreamtime:
cutleaf, gum and rowan.

They count their dead.
[54]   They can't count their dead.
The wounded sigh forever
the first letters, they
the names of the lost.

* * *

New dawn light at Brighton
shapes mountains out of darkness;
the camera's weight passes from my hands.
I imagine the meter's soft sweep
in the rectangle, her moment alone.
The sameness of the world afar
without inscape, near an eastern shore:

"Man-next-door, they've taken"
comes whimpering through the wall.

The dawn won't shrug.

Huangshan pines of many winters
reach down through ice, sparse loam
and boulder span: distant world
of seekers' gone centuries glimpsed,
and just now only, we become
the trees where moths quest.

The child's fingers wash
black earth from needles,
leaves light with dew. At once
twin equinoxes, and all around
         the mountain's breath, thought
both quantum and Cezanne's wind.

A lost icon, painter unknown:
         "This in the St. Cecilia Master . . .
                  and from Giotto. . . ."
                  And thus do we part.

Wait for sun dazzle:
         run from the doorway.
The sun will chase:
         slowly over the grass,
through oaks and empty barracks
until the shadows on the land
lift and vanish into darkness.
                  So quiet, the crickets.
The close takes you softly
to sleep, the finches relearning,
         sparrows and dreams —
                  creatures of another morning.

* * *

Sand underfoot,
no trace of home.
Fire in the glass,
no trace of sand.

The hut has home inside,
         the years placed away,
an accent of elsewhere on my tongue:

                  Many lives in moments, in mine.

From above a distant ridge,
light limns the ground
where the old tree vanished —

where a child's glance
proclaims you.